MW01104679

THE

HORSE

DEALER

For
Bridget Victoria

The Horse Dealer

by

Colleen Rutherford Archer

Colleen Rutherford Archer

Borealis Press

Ottawa, Canada

2000

The Publishers gratefully acknowledge the financial assistance of the Government of Canada through the Book Publishing Program (BPIDP), and of the Ontario Arts Council, for our publishing activities.

Canadian Cataloguing in Publication Data

Archer, Colleen Rutherford
The horse dealer

ISBN 0-88887-248-8 (bound) - ISBN 0-88887-250-X (pbk.)

1. Horses–Juvenile fiction.   I. Title.

PS8551.R36H67 2000   jC813'.54   C00-900778-4
PZ7.A6745Ho 2000

Cover design by Bull's Eye Design, Ottawa, Canada
Back cover photo by H. Brady

Printed and bound in Canada on acid free paper

Chapters

Bridle Acres   1

Chocolate   7

Jack Vargas 14

School Show 18

The Lease 24

Lucky Irish 29

Goodbye Chocolate 35

Exhibition 39

Not So Lucky 45

The Truth 49

Confrontation 54

Lesson One 60

An Old Acquaintance 65

Chapter 1

Bridle Acres

Fourteen-year-old Jean O'Brien waited patiently against a fence while her coach Jay Saunders inhaled a cigarette and watched a horse and rider in the distance. The horse and rider were jumping cross-country fences, hedges, and water-filled ditches with ease. So intent was Jay on observing them that he didn't seem to notice the slim, auburn-haired girl at his side.

"They're very good," said Jean, also directing her gaze towards nineteen-year-old Eve Pratt and her chestnut mare Miss Polly.

Jay's eyes narrowed.

"If I had $20,000 to spend on a horse, I'd be at the top of the heap too," he said, but his bitter words were barely audible.

Eve was the daughter of Louise and Charlie Pratt, owners of Bridle Acres. Her aim was to make it onto the Canadian Olympic Three Day Event team within four years, and if Miss Polly stayed sound, she felt she stood a fairly good chance of achieving her goal. She spent hours each day with the mare, leaving most of the teaching at the stable to twenty-one-year-old Jay Saunders who had been hired by her parents the year before.

Jay continued to draw on his cigarette until Eve and Miss Polly disappeared from view. Then he dropped the butt in the dirt and ground it under the heel of his leather riding boot.

"Well, I guess it's time to face the little horrors," he said, rumpling Jean's hair and smiling at her in a conspiratorial fashion. Jean didn't know anyone handsomer than Jay Saunders when he smiled.

"Am I a little horror too?" she teased.

"You, my dear, are my only hope for the spring show season. You and Chocolate have to prove to this district that I really can coach, given a rider with even a hint of athletic ability. I can yell at Sandra until the cows come home and it won't do one bit of good until she loses at least twenty pounds."

"Mike and Megan are both athletic," Jean persisted. She knew she was fishing for compliments, but she seemed unable to stop.

"That's true," said Jay. "They're also spoiled brats. Until they're willing to work, they're not going any-where, no matter how much money their parents pump into perfect little ponies. I've seen my share of snotty rich kids on the A circuit. Kids with grooms and expen-sive lessons who get on a perfectly trained pony and win ribbons simply by hanging on around a course. When I'm through with you, Jean, you'll be a horsewoman —not a passenger!"

Jean thought Jay was wonderful as a coach. Some-times the things he said about the other students were sarcastic, even cruel, but Jean knew she was different in his eyes because she worked hard and planned to make horses her career.

In the stable Sandra, Mike and Megan were tacking up ready for their lesson. Jean was there to help Jay. Often despite Jay's best instructions the others would ride clumsily, jabbing the horses in the mouth or kicking them by mistake. If the result was that the horse re-belled, Jay would put Jean on it to relax it and straighten out the problem.

Jean had begun lessons when she was eleven, start-ing with Eve who specialized in Three Day Eventing.

Although only sixteen at the time, Eve had already been a bold and accomplished rider and Jean quickly learned the basics of cross-country and stadium jumping under her direction.

Jay specialized in hunter/jumper, in which all jumping is done in a ring. After his arrival Jean switched her goal to show jumping, since Eve was now more concerned with making the Olympic team than with the students at Bridle Acres.

"How many times have I told you to tighten the girth gradually?" Jay demanded of Sandra. "Look at that pony's face. Does he look happy?"

The school pony Gem was gnashing his teeth in annoyance at the rough manner in which Sandra was tacking up. Meanwhile Mike and Megan Tarses had their matched white ponies decked out perfectly in expensive tack.

"That looks good," said Jay to the twins. "Now let's try to ride as nicely as we look."

Jean could understand why Jay lost patience with a lot of his students. Many of them weren't really serious about riding, and some of them seemed to deliberately ignore directions. Also, when left alone, some of them would canter the horse endlessly around the ring, tiring the animal out and then not cooling it off properly.

Jean always gave her half-Arab pony Chocolate the best of care, grooming her carefully both before and after riding, and warming her up properly before beginning serious work. To see a student treat a horse or pony in an inconsiderate or dangerous fashion always made her blood boil.

Jean had noticed, though, that while Jay was often curt to his students, with the parents he was consistently charming. Each time he found a horse or pony for a student or sold a horse that was no longer wanted, his ten percent commission could be added to the money he was saving to buy his own World Cup class jumping horse somewhere down the road.

"You don't need a mounting block with a pony!" Jay was screaming now at fat Sandra Roland. "If you can't get on the pony, take it back to the barn."

Red-faced, Sandra moved Gem away from the mounting block. She started to lower the stirrup on the left hand side.

"Leave the stirrup where it is," said Jay.

Jean began to feel sorry for Sandra who was fumbling now with the stirrup leather. Sandra left the iron in the position it had been, and with a great effort she raised her foot up into the stirrup.

"Now get on!"

As Sandra heaved her weight into the saddle, Gem walked off with a bit of white showing in his eye. Jean thought Sandra looked like she was about to cry.

"You shouldn't have to scramble," said Jay. "I want you to stay in the arena for an extra ten minutes after class and practise getting on and off that pony. Next week you're going to do it right, or don't bother coming. Do you understand?"

"Yes," mumbled thirteen-year-old Sandra, who had a terrible crush on Jay despite the fact that he treated her so badly.

"Mike and Megan, trot on."

The twins and Sandra actually trotted quite well, so Jean had little to do but watch for the first fifteen minutes of the lesson. It was when they got to the jumps that the trouble began.

Sandra was still upset from the beginning of the lesson. The first time she went over the crosspoles, she accidentally pulled on the reins and jabbed Gem sharply in the mouth while driving him forward with her legs.

At the next jump, rather than risk getting jabbed again, Gem stopped dead and Sandra pitched over his head onto the other side of the jump.

"Well you made it over," said Jay without the least trace of sympathy, "but you're supposed to take the horse with you. Jean, get on the pony and fix him for Sandra."

Jean caught the reluctant pony and hopped agilely onto his back while Sandra picked herself up out of the dirt.

"Take him right around," said Jay.

Jean needed lots of leg at the first jump as Gem was still afraid of being jabbed, but soon he was clearing all the jumps with no problem.

"Now get back on—properly," said Jay to Sandra, "and if you fall off again, you can clean every piece of tack in the tack room before you go home. Mike and Megan, let's see what you can do."

The ponies Jay had found for the Tarses' family were well seasoned show ponies and it took a lot to upset them. Mike came galloping around one bend incorrectly and his pony was almost parallel to the jump. Slowing right down without being asked, the pony lined himself up and took the jump from a near standstill.

"The pony saved you that time," said Jay, "but it's up to you to steer, Mike. Now it's your turn, Megan."

The ten-year-old girl went around the course without much style, but at least she was still on the pony's back and the pony itself had had no problem.

"Good," said Jay. He was never too critical in person towards the children of the very rich.

Megan's second round wasn't quite as successful. She made it around, but she took off at a long spot on the second jump and almost caused the pony to have an accident. Jay told Jean to get on the pony to demonstrate how to find the right spot for take-off.

Jean liked riding the little pony. It was trained so perfectly, it was a joy to ride. After going around twice while Jay explained what she was doing to Megan, she dismounted and gave the pony back to its owner.

When the lesson was over, Jean stayed with Sandra to help her practise mounting and dismounting.

"I don't mean to do it wrong," said Sandra, her face flushed with effort. "I wish Jay knew I'd do it right if I could."

"You'll get it with practice," said Jean kindly. "I'll hold Gem so he can't walk off, and then you only have to worry about one thing at a time."

As she gained confidence in her ability to get on without lowering the stirrup, Sandra began to land more lightly on Gem's back. Eventually the pony stopped rolling his eyes each time she began her ascent.

"I'm going to let him go now," said Jean. "If you stay calm and don't thump on him, he should stand still."

Jean stood near the pony's head to encourage him to stay put, and even though Sandra landed heavily on her first attempt, Gem didn't walk off. The second time, with her confidence increased, Sandra did much better.

"I can do it! I really can! Do you think Jay will be proud of me?"

"I'm sure he will, even if he doesn't say so," said Jean, and she wished in her heart that it were true.

Chapter Two

Chocolate

After Sandra and the Tarses twins had gone home, Jean had time to spend with her own pony Chocolate. Her parents had bought Chocolate for her when she was twelve and the pony was five.

Chocolate had belonged to a farm family and had only received very basic training. It was Jean who had taught her to trot and canter figure eights, to go calmly over trot poles, and to jump properly over both single jumps and combinations.

Jean was grooming her now, ready for a training session in the arena. Carefully she picked out her hooves and then she began to brush her, working her way from front to back.

"That's my good girl," she crooned, and the pony lowered her head in appreciation.

"I wish somebody cared about me like you care about that pony."

The speaker was Dennis Gentry, the pale, long-haired stable boy recently hired by the Pratts at minimum wage to clean stalls. Jay called him a "mall rat," and Jean wasn't sure if she trusted the gangly youth or not.

"Hi Dennis. How are you doing?"

"Okay, I guess. Except this job is pretty boring. Jay is teaching me how to groom, though, and when I get good enough, he's going to let me groom all the horses every day when I finish the stalls."

Dennis looked so proud as he pushed his wheelbarrow past Chocolate that Jean felt she'd better say

7

something.

"That's great, Dennis. There are always lots of jobs available for good grooms."

"Groom. Hey, I like that. Occupation—groom!"

Dennis grinned as he headed to the back stall. Jean was glad when he was busy mucking out and she didn't have to think of anything else to say to him.

"How's it going, kid?"

"Pretty good."

Jean smiled up at Jay who had come in to fetch Candy, a new bay Thoroughbred the Pratts had just purchased for the school.

"Say, how'd you like to get Candy ready while I have a smoke outside? Then we can ride together. What time are your parents picking you up?"

"Whenever I phone," said Jean, who was anxious to get started with Chocolate but always found it hard to say no to any of Jay's requests.

"Good. I'll be back in fifteen minutes. That should give you lots of time."

Jean left Chocolate in the crossties while she groomed Candy. Then she tacked up both the horse and pony and stood waiting for Jay to return. It was well over fifteen minutes and Candy was getting restless.

She led the Thoroughbred into a stall and stood on tiptoe and peered out the window to see if Jay was almost done with his cigarette. She saw him over by his truck, but he wasn't alone. Sheila Graham, one of his older students, was with him and he had his arm around her shoulders. As Sheila got into her sports car, Jay gave her a long kiss goodbye.

When Jay came back into the barn, Jean was in the aisle holding both Choclate and Candy.

"Hurry up," she said with some irritation. "It's not easy holding two horses at once."

"Sorry. After I finished my cigarette, I discovered one of the fence rails was down and I had to fix it."

"I saw you with Sheila," said Jean matter-of-factly. Jay laughed.

"Oh oh. Caught in the act. Sheila's a real pain," said Jay. "She calls all the horses 'cute' and she giggles through all her lessons. She supposedly stopped by to pay for last week's lesson, and it's part of my job, you know, to keep the customers satisfied."

The look on his face was totally unrepentant. Then suddenly he looked worried.

"You won't tell Eve, will you?"

Jay had been trying to romance Eve since his arrival at Bridle Acres, but Eve had little time for such nonsense.

"Of course not," said Jean indignantly. "What do you think I am? A tattletale?"

"That's my girl. Now let's get riding!"

Candy had been bought off the race track and Jay wanted to retrain her in the least time possible for use in the school. In the arena he attached a tight martingale to her bridle (a strap passing from the noseband to the girth between the forelegs) to keep her head down. Jean had seen him ride a horse the same way many times before trying to sell it, removing the martingale at the last possible moment. The potential buyers would then see a false head set and think the horse was better educated than it actually was.

"I'll have this horse ready for lessons in two weeks," he bragged now.

The horse was full of resistance, but Jay was an extremely calm and talented rider and soon he had the horse circling the arena in what appeared to be an obedient manner.

Meanwhile Jean was warming up Chocolate, doing

a lot of trot circles and figure eights. The pony had come a long way in the past two years and Jean was looking forward to the summer show season. The school's own show was the last Saturday in May, only two short weeks away, but Jean knew there would be little competition for Chocolate there.

"Set up some jumps," said Jay. "Let's see how this horse reacts."

Jean knew Candy should go through a long process of training with trot poles before attempting a jump, but she did as she was told.

"Not too high," said Jay. "Just a couple of feet."

Jean left Chocolate standing with the reins over her head while she set up two jumps, one on each long side of the arena. That was one of the things she liked best about her pony. They had become good buddies, and Jean felt she could trust Chocolate completely not to walk away when told to stay.

"You go around first," said Jay.

Jean remounted and picked up a canter from a halt. Chocolate glided over the jumps, going only as high as was necessary to clear the two foot height.

"Well done," said Jay approvingly. "I must admit, I'm one fantastic coach."

Jay picked up a canter to the left around a bend and headed for the first jump. When Candy saw the jump, she tried to raise her head in terror but the martingale held it down. As she reached the jump, she went straight up in the air and came down heavily on the other side, galloping for all she was worth.

"Whoa there," said Jay soothingly, pulling back firmly on the reins. Eventually he got her down to a trot, and finally a fast walk. Then he started to laugh.

"The old kangaroo jump," he said. "Never mind. She'll catch on fast enough."

Jean knew that was true. Jay seemed to be able to make a horse look good around a hunter ring in an amazingly short space of time. She wondered if some day she would be able to train as quickly and effectively.

"How's it going, Jay?"

The speaker was Eve Pratt who had just come back from taking Miss Polly on a conditioning ride up and down the hills behind the farm. She stood now beside the horse, peering over the bars at the open end of the arena.

"Fine." Jay's eyes narrowed, as they always seemed to do in Eve's presence. "She'll be stiff to the right for awhile after tearing around a track to the left for years, but we'll soon fix that."

"Don't you think that martingale's a bit tight?"

"I just put it on her," lied Jay, "and I haven't really adjusted it. She was having some trouble keeping her head down, so I thought we'd better use it for a few minutes to help give her the idea what to do."

"Loosen it at least two notches," said Eve, and she walked off, leading Miss Polly towards the barn.

"Loosen it at least two notches," imitated Jay, and then he winked at Jean.

"If she had to train the number of horses and people I have to train, she'd use a few gadgets too. She spends all her time with the wonder horse Miss Polly. I have to work with twenty-six students, plus every new horse that comes on the place."

Jean began to wonder if her old friend Eve might be a bit of a tyrant.

They walked Candy and Chocolate until they were cool, then took them back to the barn. While they were removing the saddles and bridles and brushing away the saddle marks, Jean talked to Chocolate constantly and petted her. Then she got her an apple from her tack box.

"You shouldn't spoil a horse, you know," said Jay. "It doesn't pay to get too attached to them. If you want to show at the top levels, you're going to be riding a lot of horses. Getting attached to them will only stand in your way."

"But I love Chocolate," said Jean. Jay turned his back and became engrossed in picking out Candy's hooves. When he faced her again, he wasn't smiling.

"Do you want to be a show jumper, Jean?"

"Of course I do."

"Then grow up."

That was all he said, and Jean felt shocked and a little hurt.

After he put Candy in her stall, Jay returned and rumpled Jean's hair. His smile was back, and his blue eyes were warm and sincere.

"You don't have to worry about any of that for awhile, kid," he said. "Just worry about getting Chocolate ready for our schooling show. We're going to beat the pants off every kid in this district. Right?"

"Right."

Jean was constantly torn between her desire to please Jay and to win, and her dislike of the way Jay seemed to take pleasure in the misfortune of other riders. Often it seemed nothing made him happier that to see a rival fall off a horse at a show.

She put Chocolate in her stall now, giving her one last hand rub and kissing her on the forehead before she said goodbye.

"Have you got a kiss for me too?"

Jean jumped, for she hadn't heard Dennis Gentry come up behind her.

"Do you have to sneak up on people like that?"

"I'll bet you'd have a kiss for me if I had a blonde

moustache and blue eyes, and if my name were Jay Saunders."

"Don't be stupid, Dennis. You'd better behave yourself, or I'll tell Mr. Pratt."

Dennis immediately backed off.

"Please don't, Jean. I was only teasing."

Dennis had been unemployed for a long time, and he didn't want to risk the only job he had seemed able to get. He started sweeping the barn floor with great energy, and Jean picked up her saddle pad and cloth girth which she wanted to take home to wash. She had already phoned her father, and she decided she would be more comfortable waiting for him outside.

After she had gone, Dennis began muttered to himself:

"He may not kiss you, Jean, but he kisses all the older ones behind the barn."

Dennis genuinely liked and admired Jean, but he hated Jay Saunders.

Chapter Three

Jack Vargas

The Sunday before the school show, Jean had just finished exercising Chocolate when Jack Vargas walked in. The Pratts let Jay bring horses in and out of the barn to sell, and Mr. Vargas was his chief supplier. Dennis pushed past Jean and Chocolate in the aisleway, stopping long enough to whisper:

"Straight as a dog's hind leg." Then he hurried on with his pitchfork, since if he cleaned all the stalls on Sundays, he got time and a half.

Jean agreed with Dennis. The Pratts were rarely around when Mr. Vargas arrived, but Jean had seen the dealings that went on. She had also seen the vials, bottles and needles in the back of Mr. Vargas's truck, and she knew that drugs were often used to disguise problems in the horses Mr. Vargas transported.

"What have you got for me today?" asked Jay cheerfully, coming from Candy's stall.

"Just the two," said Mr. Vargas. "Both off the track. You can have them for a thousand each. One had a slight fracture in the knee, but you'd never know it when you ride him now. Unless the buyer has an X-ray done, you're home free."

"And the other?"

"A little stiff in the stifles. Bute him up a bit, and he'll pass."

"And when the bute wears off?"

"You don't know anything about it. Must have hap-

14

pened after you sold him."

"What do you think I'll make?"

"You could whip these two into shape within the month and sell them for three, maybe four thousand."

Jean felt a little uncomfortable overhearing this conversation, but Jay had often told her how difficult it was to make a dollar in the horse industry, and that when it came to sales it was universally understood that it was "buyer beware." His only loyalty, he told her, was to his serious students. Now Jay turned to Mr. Vargas.

"Let's get them unloaded, then. Jean! Put Chocolate away and give us a hand."

Jean would like to have been asked to help instead of told, but she put Chocolate away without comment. Then she followed Jay and Jack Vargas outside.

The trailer Mr. Vargas used was old and rickety without safety brakes. Another thing Jean disliked about it was that there was no unloading ramp so the horses had to step down onto the ground through empty space.

The two Thoroughbreds were sad-eyed and bony. Often when horses failed to make it at one of the smaller tracks they were deserted, as that was cheaper than taking them away. Jean wondered if that's what had happened to this pair.

"They look kind of scrawny," she said to Jay.

"Don't worry about that. We'll pump them full of grain and you won't recognize them in a month."

The first horse was extremely tall so he looked even skinnier than his mate. His hooves were pared down so far that it looked like it must hurt him to walk.

"What's the matter with his feet?" asked Jean.

"Abscesses," said Mr. Vargas. "The farrier had to cut them away. His hooves will have grown by the time Jay wants to sell him."

With Jay guiding him, the chestnut gelding leapt

backwards off the trailer and then erupted. Jean jumped back to avoid his flying hooves.

"Whoa boy!"

Jay pulled sharply on the lead rope and calmed the sweating beast. Then he held the rope out to Jean.

"Here you go. Put him in the back stall in the west wing."

Unwilling to show she was afraid, Jean took the rope and said with all the conviction she could muster:

"Walk on!"

Prancing and dancing, the horse came along beside her on his tender hooves.

Jean was relieved when she got the animal safely into his stall. There fresh water, hay and grain awaited him.

"I hope Jay doesn't expect me to turn that sucker out," said Dennis, who had watched Jean bring the new horse in.

"I doubt if he'll get out much," said Jean. "He needs some time for his hooves to heal."

She wondered what the chestnut's temperament would be like in two weeks' time locked in a dark stall on high feed.

"Jean!"

Jay had the second horse unloaded—a kind-eyed bay with good conformation. All he needed was fattening up and he'd be a fine looking animal.

"Is this the one that's stiff in the stifles?" asked Jean.

"Forget you ever heard that," said Jay with a wink. "There's no such thing as a perfect horse, you know. They've all got something wrong with them."

"I like him," said Jean. "Did he win many races?"

"Never won a single one," said Mr. Vargas. "Never even placed. I guess he liked to watch the other horses running by."

"Maybe he's like Ferdinand," said Jean. "He'd rather smell the flowers. I think that's what I'll call him. Ferdinand."

"Call him whatever you want," said Jay with a shrug. "Just get him into his stall."

Ferdinand was well-behaved as Jean let him into the barn and put him into the waiting stall.

"At least he gets a window," she said to Dennis. "I like this one."

"Looks like all the others to me," said Dennis. "A brown horse. Don't Thoroughbreds come in any colour but brown?"

"What about that grey mare Jay sold to the Moores last week?"

"Oh yeah. I had to hit her once with a pitchfork when she turned on me while I was cleaning her stall. Jay sold her to a woman for her eleven-year-old daughter. The daughter thought the mare was cute."

Cute.

Jean remembered that Sheila had thought the mare was cute too. She thought of Jay kissing Sheila. Then she thought of the woman and her eleven-year-old daughter, and she hoped the grey mare hadn't turned on either of them while they were cleaning out her stall.

Chapter Four

School Show

When Jean awoke the May Sunday morning of the Bridle Acres school show she was happy to discover it was bright and sunny outside.

"I'm not coming!"

Her ten-year-old brother's screech from the kitchen reached her all the way upstairs. She could hear her mother trying to reason with Jason, although she couldn't make out exactly what she was saying. Jean leapt out of bed and ran downstairs to join in the fray.

"I don't want him coming anyways. All he does is embarrass me. Can't he stay at Billy's?"

"Billy's family has gone away for the weekend. Besides, he should come and watch you compete. You go to all his hockey games."

"Big deal," said Jason. "I don't ask her to go to my games, do I?"

"What's the problem, Ruth?" asked Mr. O'Brien, coming in and pouring himself a cup of coffee.

"Jason doesn't want to go to the horse show."

"I thought you liked horses," said Mr. O'Brien to his son.

"I do like horses. It's Jean and her creepy friends I don't like."

"That's enough!" said Mrs. O'Brien looking suddenly very tired, and Jean began to feel sorry for her.

"I'll tell you what, pig face," she said to Jason. "If you come and behave yourself, I'll let you take Choco-

18

late on the trails after the show. Deal?"

"Deal!"

Jason finished shoveling in his cereal and toast and ran to his room to get dressed.

"Are you sure he'll be safe?" asked Mrs. O'Brien.

"Chocolate will take care of him. Besides, I'll borrow one of the school ponies and go along. Jay doesn't like anyone going out on the trails alone."

"Jay seems like a very sensible and nice young man," said Mr. O'Brien. "The Pratts are lucky to have found him.

"What time do we have to leave?"

"My first class is at ten," said Jean, "and I'll need at least an hour to get Chocolate ready, so we should leave here in half an hour."

She ate a quick breakfast and then gathered up the equipment she had prepared the night before including the freshly oiled and polished saddle, bridle, and girth, and the clean show saddle pad.

The list of necessary items seemed endless: hunter crop, rug hook and wool for braiding, riding hat and cover, white shirt, collar, pin, jacket, breeches, boots, gloves, towel for cleaning boots, and boot polish. Still, it wasn't as bad as a show you trailered to when you also needed to take along brushes, a hoof pick, sweat scraper, horse cooler and blanket, buckets, feed, water, extra halters, lead ropes, sponges, and fly spray. All those things were safely stored at the barn.

When they arrived at Bridle Acres there were already lots of cars, trucks and horse trailers there. The show was open to outside riders and lots of 4H and Pony Club children had brought their horses and ponies for the day.

"Looks like there's going to be a big turnout," said Mr. O'Brien. "Louise and Charlie certainly picked the right day this year. This is the warmest day we've had all spring."

They headed to the barn, which was a beehive of activity.

"Hi Jean. Ready to go out there and win?" Jay was helping some of the smaller children get their ponies ready for the novice class.

"I don't know. There are a lot of horse trailers out there."

"Amateurs. If you can't beat the people from around here after all my coaching, I'll retire today."

While Jean got Chocolate groomed and tacked up ready for the Junior Division, Mr. and Mrs. O'Brien watched the Novice Division. Mrs. O'Brien liked the lead line class where little children were led around by their older brothers and sisters. She applauded loudly for the first place winner—a tiny, red-haired girl on a big sorrel mare.

"Jack. Where's Jason gone?" she asked, when her favorite class was over.

"To the snack bar," said Mr. O'Brien. "Where else?"

In the novice pleasure class the Tarses twins took first and second place. In novice equitation where it was the rider's position that was being judged, a boy from another stable took first place and the twins didn't even place.

Sandra Roland rode Gem in the novice command. Gem was so used to these classes that he executed the judge's commands almost before Sandra had time to cue him. One by one the other competitors were eliminated, and in the end Sandra was awarded the first place ribbon.

When Sandra ran into the barn pulling Gem behind her, her round cheeks were flushed with pride. Excitedly she waved her red ribbon for Jean and Jay to see.

"Congratulations!" said Jean, giving the younger girl a quick hug.

"What class?" asked Jay.

"Novice command."

"Well there's one for the pony," he said dryly.

The light went out of Sandra's eyes and Jean was so mad at Jay she could have kicked him.

"That was really rotten," she said after Sandra had taken Gem back to his stall. "You saw how excited she was about getting a ribbon."

"You're right," said Jay. "I just get so tired of all the novices demanding so much time and attention. I'll tell you what. I'll go and make amends right now."

He headed off towards Gem's stall and when Sandra came back with her ribbon clutched tightly in her hand, her eyes were shining. She looked at Jean who was putting a braid in Chocolate's tail.

"You know, if my parents could afford to buy me a good pony, I'd probably get an invitation to the Royal!"

Sandra shot Jean a triumphant glance and then she ran outside to show her ribbon to her admiring parents. Jean laughed inwardly at the thought of fat Sandra at the Royal.

"Satisfied?"

Jay's eyes were mocking.

"I guess. How come you have to lie to be nice, Jay?"

"Because in most cases the truth hurts. Not with you, though. You're darn good, and we both know it. Now get out there. They're calling for junior hunter hack."

There were five classes in the junior division— hunter hack, equitation on the flat, working hunter over fences, handy hunter over fences, and equitation over fences. Most of the riders were older than Jean, some on large horses, but Jean and Chocolate made a clean sweep of first place in all five classes. Dennis Gentry had come out from the barn to watch admiringly.

"Fantastic, honey!" said Mr. O'Brien, taking Jean's

and Chocolate's picture with their array of ribbons.

"Do I get my ride now?" whined Jason. "This whole day was boring."

"If you're bored, I have a horse that could give you a mighty good ride," said Jay. "His name's Rodney. He's a tall chestnut Thoroughbred right off the track."

"Wow. Could I ride him, Mum?" He shoved the remains of his fifth chocolate bar of the day into his shirt pocket.

"Don't tempt her," said Jay, winking at Mrs. O'Brien, and she smiled back wearily at the handsome young man.

"You take the wonder pony Chocolate while she's all tacked up, Jason," said Jay, "and don't forget to borrow a hat from the tack room. You can use Gem, Jean. He's finished for the day."

"Thanks Jay," said Jean.

"But I want to ride the race horse," said Jason, "and I don't want to wear a hat."

Jean handed him Chocolate's reins and said, "You have to wear a hat or you don't ride."

Jason was going to protest further, but one look at his father's face made him decide against it.

As soon as the youngsters had disappeared, Jay took a position between Jack and Ruth O'Brien and began to talk to them in a low and serious voice.

"You know, Jean's too good for a pony now," he said, looking deeply into Mrs. O'Brien's eyes. "You saw her here today. Why she could go into the Open right now and beat all the adults if Chocolate were big enough to do the jumps."

"A horse? She's only fourteen and she's small," said Mr. O'Brien. "I figured the pony would do her another couple of years."

"Age and size have nothing to do with it," said Jay,

trying to keep any hint of annoyance out of his voice. "It's ability that counts, and Jean has it."

He gazed into the ring where Sheila Graham was just starting a hunter round on the Thoroughbred Candy. "Darn her," said Jay angrily. "I told her she wasn't ready to jump. So what does she do? She rents the horse from Eve for the day and puts herself into working hunter. I'd like to—"

He seemed to recall whom he was with and didn't finish his sentence. Deliberately he forced his tense muscles to relax.

At the first jump Candy refused and Sheila was dumped unceremoniously on the ground. She picked herself up and remounted. Hitting the horse viciously with the crop, she came at the jump again. This time the fall was harder and Mrs. O'Brien gasped.

"I hope she hasn't hurt herself."

Jay didn't answer. Nor did he go to see Sheila after the officials had helped her up off the ground and led her out of the ring.

"Jean could get around that course on Candy right now with no problem whatsoever," said Jay to Mr. and Mrs. O'Brien. "Think about it. Every young rider has to move up from a pony to a horse at some stage in his or her career. It's never an easy transition, but waiting certainly doesn't make it any easier."

With a nod of farewell, he headed off towards the barn.

Chapter Five

The Lease

Jay was waiting for Jean when she biked up to the stable Monday after school.

"I've found him!" he said, his eyes shining.

"Found who?"

"The perfect horse for you. I was up at Bartons' Equestrian Centre in Toronto this morning trying out a mare for a client who wants a Connemara pony. While I was trying out the pony, Fred brought in a seven-year-old Thoroughbred gelding for another buyer. You should see him, Jean! He's just what you need."

"I don't think my parents are ready to buy me a horse yet," said Jean, thinking of her beloved Chocolate.

"They could be persuaded," said Jay.

"Every young rider has to leave a pony behind at some point and move up to a horse," he added, almost as if he could read her mind.

"But what would happen to Chocolate? We don't have a buyer for her, and I know Mom and Dad can't afford to pay board on two horses."

"I didn't want to mention this until the right horse came along, but I have a cousin Frances near Burlington who loves horses, and her little girl is a crackerjack rider. They couldn't afford to pay much, but Chocolate would have a good home. By selling her right away instead of waiting for a high price, you'd save board and probably come out ahead in the long run."

"I don't know. I'd have to think about it."

"I'm afraid there's no time to think about it. The other buyer wants that horse, but since Fred and I have been pals since grade school, he told me if I want him, I can take him tomorrow. If he's still there Wednesday, he's sold. I tell you, Jean, the horse is a steal at three thousand."

"Three thousand dollars? I don't think I can persuade my parents to pay that much, even if it is a good price. Besides, first you'd have to convince them that I really need a horse right now and not a pony."

"No problem."

Jay arrived at the O'Brien home right after dinner with photographs of the bay gelding Lucky Irish in a file folder which also contained his passport. The passport was stamped with all the recognized shows the horse had attended.

"Fred lent me this until tomorrow," said Jay. "I know it's a big decision to make in such a hurry, but a horse like this comes along once in a lifetime. I look at dozens of horses every week, and I know this horse is right for Jean."

"You say he's three thousand dollars?" asked Mr. O'Brien, trying to take it all in.

"And worth twice that. I wouldn't even take a commission on this sale, Jack. I just want Jean to have that horse. She deserves it."

Jean couldn't help but feel flattered at Jay's faith in her abilities.

"Three thousand dollars is an awful lot of money," said Mrs. O'Brien. "Besides, we can't afford the board on two horses."

"I've already discussed that with Jean," said Jay. "I have an excellent home for Chocolate. The people can't afford much - only a thousand dollars - but by selling her right away you could be saving months of board and vet bills on her. Ponies can be awfully hard to sell."

"That leaves two thousand dollars," said Mr. O'Brien. "I guess we could afford that, if Jean's really as good as you say she is, but there's no way I'm buying a pig in a poke."

"What's a pig in a poke?" demanded Jason.

"That means a pig in a sack or a bag," said his father. "The expression means you wouldn't buy something you haven't seen or tried out."

Jay's eyes narrowed momentarily; then he relaxed and smiled.

"Well, I guess I can't really blame you for that. But how about this?

"One way or another I want that horse in the barn. If you don't want him, I'll buy him myself and you can lease him for regular board fee. If you decide you don't want to buy him, you can buy a different horse at any time, or just cancel the board agreement."

"Sounds fair to me," said Mr. O'Brien. "What do you think, Ruth?"

"Well, I don't see what we've got to lose. We'll just be paying the same board we're paying now."

"And I'll even give you a cheque for Chocolate tonight," said Jay. "I trust my cousin Frances to give me the money! Then I'll go and buy Lucky Irish from Fred in the morning, and he'll be waiting for Jean when she comes up after school."

"Can I fix you a drink, Jay?" asked Mr. O'Brien. "I think I could use one right about now."

"Just juice or a soft drink, please," said Jay.

"Ruth?"

"I'll have some juice too, please."

"I guess that's five juices, then," said Mr. O'Brien, heading for the kitchen. He didn't like to drink alone.

As soon as he had gone, Jay sat closer to Jean's

mom.

"Ruth," he said. "I've bought and sold a lot of horses in my time and I don't usually get excited about any particular one. This time it's different. Jean is my best student and Lucky Irish is the best horse I've seen for a long time. I can hardly wait to get the two of them together. I know I'm going to have a combination that can make it to the Royal."

Remembering Sandra, Jean felt a little uncomfortable at the mention of the Royal. Her mother was obviously impressed, however.

"It's certainly good of you to give her the opportunity to ride such a horse. I'm still a little concerned about Chocolate's price, though. If she does well at a few of the bigger shows this summer, she should go for a lot more than a thousand dollars. We paid that much for her untrained."

"You're right about the price," said Jay. "I probably could get more for you in the summer. The big advantage in selling to my cousin, though, is that you know what kind of home Chocolate is going to. Frances never sells her animals, either. If you sell to someone on the circuit, you never know where the horse or pony is going to eventually end up."

"I don't want Chocolate to go to just anybody," said Jean pleadingly. "Please don't sell her to just anybody."

"Pumpkin, I think your mother's right," said Mr. O'Brien, putting a tray covered in drinks and biscuits down on the coffee table. Jason went to work on the biscuits at once. "A thousand dollars is not very much for a pony of Chocolate's caliber."

"That's true, Jack," said Jay, leaning back on the chesterfield. "Don't forget, though, that if you sell her in, let's say, August, you'll have paid another four hundred dollars board on her, plus show expenses, vet bills and another shoeing. At the moment, too, she's going well and she's going sound. It's always when you're trying to sell a horse that it pulls a ligament, or gets tangled in a fence, or falls into a groundhog hole."

"Well I don't know what to think," said Mrs. O'Brien. "It's up to you, Jack."

"Please let her go where we know she'll be getting a good home, Dad," said Jean.

"I suppose that *is* worth a lot," said Mr. O'Brien with a sigh. "Give us the cheque, then, Jay, and you've got yourself a deal."

Jay wrote the cheque and turned it over, and Mr. O'Brien told Jean to go and get Chocolate's papers. He was sorry the pony would be leaving, but he was glad to know his talented daughter would soon have a full-sized horse to ride.

Despite her happiness at the thought of having a Throughbred to jump, there was a large lump in Jean's throat as she handed over Chocolate's file to Jay. She had been well-aware since she first started riding that all competitive riders had to eventually give up their out-grown ponies for a horse, but logic couldn't stop the tears from rolling down her cheeks that night after she went upstairs to her room to bed.

Chapter Six

Lucky Irish

Jean pedaled as fast as she could to the barn Tuesday after school. Her dad would pick her up as usual when he finished work, throwing her bike into the back of the van he had bought, instead of a new car, so that he could pull a horse trailer to the shows.

Chocolate had become a family hobby. Now the leased horse Lucky Irish would become their pet instead.

"Where is he?" she asked excitedly, dropping her bike outside and running into the barn.

"You mean the new nag, I presume," said Dennis Gentry slowly. "He's in Rodney's old stall, and that's a good place for him. He's a mean one too."

"Mean?"

"Yeah. Worse than Rodney, if you ask me. Tried to sidekick me when I put him away."

"What happened to Rodney?"

Jean had never particularly liked the tall chestnut, but she wouldn't want anything bad to happen to any horse.

"Jay took him when he went to pick up your new horse. I think he sold him to someone he met at Fred's."

Dennis continued mechanically sweeping the aisle, pushing the bits of straw and manure into Candy's open stall.

"Jay's quite a wheeler-dealer if you ask me," he added.

"Where is he now?"

29

"Teaching a lesson. He said to tell you if you wanted to try out Lucky Irish, to groom him and tack him up and he'd give you a hand after he finishes with Cindy and Susan. You be careful, though, Jean."

"Who are Cindy and Susan?"

"Two new students. Just started today. Good lookers, too."

Jean had been hoping Jay would be there when she first met her new horse. After what Dennis had said, she approached Lucky Irish's stall with some apprehension. She peered into the darkness and leapt back as Irish stormed the door, his ears back and his teeth bared.

"Jay says that's just a mannerism," said Dennis. "Looks like more than a mannerism to me."

Slowly Jean eased the door open and snapped a lead shank onto the horse's ragged halter. Then she led him out and put him in cross-ties ready to be groomed.

When she looked at Lucky Irish, she almost cried. Instead of being sleekly firm like her little mare, the large gelding was bony and obviously out of condition. His eye showed white in the corner, and his hooves were dry and ragged.

"Are you sure this is Lucky Irish?" she asked Dennis. "He doesn't look like the horse in the picture Jay gave us."

"It's him all right. Jay says he hasn't been used for awhile and he's out of shape. He said to tell you not to worry. He'll have the horse in top condition in no time. It seems that Lucky Irish has a lot of training and showing behind him, but his owner hasn't had time to use him lately so he put him on just hay and no grain.

"That's Jay's story, anyways."

"What do you mean, `That's Jay's story.' Don't you believe him?"

"Why would I believe him?" said Dennis. "I know

you like to think Jay wouldn't lie to you, but a fox is a fox and not a lap dog."

When Jean tried to go over Lucky Irish with the rubber curry brush, the horse gnashed his teeth and twisted his head. At one point he raised a back leg threateningly. Nervously Jean switched to a soft brush, but the horse still seemed bothered by the slightest touch.

When the horse was reasonably clean, Jean slowly eased a saddle onto his back. Lucky Irish's tail swished violently back and forth and he raised his head. As gently as she could, she tightened the girth one notch at a time. The horse objected to every movement.

The bridle was no easier to get on than the saddle, and Jean breathed a sigh of relief when Irish was finally ready. On the way out, she stopped to talk to Ferdinand.

"You're a good boy," she crooned to the bay, who was almost identical in colour to her new horse. "Maybe we should buy you instead, even if you are a bit stiff in the stifles."

Ferdinand nickered softly at her, while Lucky Irish barged out the barn door.

In the arena Jay was obviously enjoying himself teasing his new students Cindy and Susan. The two friends had never ridden before and he had them on stalwart school horses named Jake and Buddy. The teenagers were obviously enjoying themselves immensely, giggling and carrying on. Both wore heavy make-up, and they seemed to Jean to be vying for Jay's attention and not paying much attention to the horses underneath them at all.

"Oh Jean, hi. Meet Cindy and Susan. They just started today, so you'll have to show them how it's done."

"Hello."

Jean walked her new horse into the centre of the

ring, let down her stirrups, and mounted. The teens eyed her as if she were some sort of intruder, not saying a word.

"This is our new horse Lucky Irish," said Jay. "He's a little out of shape, but he's got super conformation and he's going to take Jean right to the top."

Jean walked Irish around the arena several times, then asked him for a trot. After two rounds at a trot, the horse was wheezing and trying to come back to a walk.

"Keep him going," said Jay. "If he doesn't go forward with your leg, use the crop. Only ask him once with your leg."

Jean felt sorry for the horse, since it was obvious his not going forward was due to a lack of physical fitness rather than obstinacy.

"Use your crop!"

Jean gave him a tap behind the saddle and Irish momentarily went faster, then faded. She could hear Cindy whispering to Susan,

"*She's* going to show us how it's done?"

"Cindy and Susan," said Jay. "Cool out your horses and then take them back to the barn. Dennis will show you how to untack them and groom them before putting them away."

"Why do we have to groom them before putting them away?" asked Susan. "We groomed them before we got on."

"The best time to groom horses is after exercise. It also gives you a chance to check for any signs of swelling or lameness. If I find any saddle marks on them when I finish in here, I'll have to take stern measures with you both next week."

"Ooh," said Susan in a silly voice. "And what do you propose to do?"

"Believe me, you don't want to know," said Jay with

a wink.

Jean hated it when Jay played games with his female students. To her, riding was serious business. The girls she admired most were those who took riding seriously and had no time for Jay's fooling around - girls like Eve.

Cindy and Susan took as long as they possibly could to walk out their mounts, and it seemed to Jean they deliberately got in her way as much as possible. At last Jay said,

"That's good enough, girls. Don't forget what I said about grooming the horses before you put them away."

"We'll *try* to remember," said Susan. "See you next week."

"Be good," said Cindy. "Until next week, that is."

Jean was relieved when they were finally gone and she could concentrate on Lucky Irish.

"What a couple of bimboes," said Jay.

"You don't have to lead them on."

"What's this? A lecture on morality from a fourteen-year-old?"

"It's just that they don't seem very interested in riding."

"You're absolutely right. They're here because their friend Jenny, who used to take lessons at Bridle Acres, told them about me. They plan to come once a week and want mainly to enjoy themselves. At twenty dollars each, that means forty dollars into the school for a fairly easy hour during which I can train one of my own horses. It's economics, my dear. Strictly economics."

"You aren't training a horse right now."

"That's because I was waiting for you. When I do come across an actual rider, I take him or her very seriously. Understand?"

"Yes."

"Now let's see a canter."

Jean asked Lucky Irish to canter, and on the first turn to the left the horse stumbled and she felt her neck snap. The horse recovered and she didn't fall off, but the pain shot right from her neck down between her shoulders.

"He doesn't exactly bend, does he?" Jay didn't sound particularly worried. "I know what he does do, though, and that's jump."

He set up a fence about three-and-a-half feet high.

"Bring him around to this."

As soon as Lucky Irish saw the jump, his ears pricked up and he forgot he was winded. His canter stride increased and he sailed over the jump while Jean fought for control.

Jay laughed.

"Well, what do you think now?"

"He can sure clear a fence."

Jean tried to ignore the pain in her neck that was threatening to bring tears to her eyes.

"This boy will be doing four-and-a-half feet in no time," said Jay.

"He seems a little lacking in basics and manners, though," said Jean, dismounting and leading Irish around the arena. She couldn't keep her disappointment to herself any longer.

"Don't worry about that, Jean. I won't desert you with him. I promise we'll have him ready for the show ring before the Fairview exhibition, and that's only the end of June."

He put his arm around her shoulders and gave her a friendly hug.

"Have I ever led you wrong before?"

Chapter Seven

Goodbye Chocolate

The Saturday after Lucky Irish arrived was the day Chocolate was to be taken to Burlington, and Jean bicycled to Bridle Acres at dawn to say goodbye. She was the only one in the barn as she hugged her dear friend and told her how much she was going to miss her. In a few short hours the students and stable helpers would arrive.

"You're the best pony in the whole world," Jean told Chocolate, feeding the pony pieces of apple and carrot and stroking her velvet nose. Chocolate whinnied her appreciation, while Lucky Irish screamed from his stall. Chocolate rubbed her teeth against the wires of her door at the sound of the big gelding.

Chocolate hated Lucky Irish with a passion, since for the past few days he had been taking all of Jean's attention whenever she was at the barn. By the time Jean finished grooming and schooling the difficult horse, there seemed to be little energy left for schooling the pony who now belonged to someone else. During their daily turnout in the big field Chocolate would run at Irish and nip his flanks, then whirl and scurry away at top speed before he could retaliate.

Sadly Jean began to groom the pony one last time. She brushed Chocolate in her stall; something she wouldn't dare to try with Irish. Even in cross-ties Irish was difficult to groom, grinding his teeth and biting at the ties.

"Hit him when he does that," commanded Jay. "Sooner or later he'll get tired of being thumped."

Reluctantly Jean did as she was told, but it only seemed to make matters worse. Still, Jay must know what worked best since he had trained so many horses.

Chocolate stood completely still while Jean picked up each of her feet in turn and carefully picked them out.

"You're such a good girl," said Jean. "Too bad you can't teach Irish how to behave."

Several times that week Irish had threatened to kick Jean while she picked out his back feet. Once Jay had been in the barn.

"This isn't your precious little pony," he had said with a hard edge in his voice. "You're going to have to show him who's boss, or he's going to show you."

That night Jean had been close to tears. She considered telling her parents about the trouble she was having with the new horse, but in the end she decided to wait and see how things progressed. How could she tell them so soon that she disliked the big horse, and that she wished she had kept her lovely pony Chocolate? She would just have to believe Jay was right about Irish.

At eight o'clock Dennis arrived at the barn. He worked for awhile in silence, glancing over occasionally at Jean, and then he said:

"She's a real nice pony. She'll be okay."

Jean smiled at him appreciatively, and he began to whistle happily as he fed the horses their hay and measured out their grain.

At quarter to nine Jay showed up, ready for his first students of the day.

"How's my girl?" he said to Jean softly, and his eyes seemed kind and understanding.

"I'm fine."

Jean didn't want to display any of the softness that

she knew from past experience might cause Jay to turn hard and cold. Today she needed all the help she could get from everyone.

"The trailer's coming about eleven," said Jay. "I have a completely full lesson schedule, but I'll be out to help load, I promise."

"Thanks," said Jean. "I've never had to say goodbye forever to a friend before."

"My cousin will take good care of Chocolate," said Jay. "Don't you worry about that. I know it's hard the first time you have to sell a horse, but you'll get used to it. You'll see."

Jean wasn't sure she wanted to get used to it, but she didn't dare say that to Jay.

At five minutes after eleven the trailer arrived. Jean had been expecting a one-horse trailer and possibly a worn, old pick-up truck, since Jay's cousin's family didn't have much money. Instead the trailer was an impressive four-horse gooseneck complete with grooming room, and the truck was shiny new.

A well-attired man of about fifty stepped out of the truck, accompanied by a tall young woman in cream breeches, a vest and riding boots.

The man approached Jean and asked politely:

"Pardon me, miss, but do you know where I might find a Mr. Jay Saunders?"

Before Jean could answer, Jay came hastily out of the arena.

"You go in the barn and get Chocolate," he said to Jean. "I'll handle things here."

Jean already had Chocolate's legs bandaged ready for her journey. Now she led her out to the driveway where Jay was talking in low tones to the man and girl.

"You can load her if you like, Jean," Jay said much more loudly. Then he turned to the man.

"Chocolate loads like a breeze. Jean has done a super job with her in all areas."

By the time the pony was loaded, Jay had shaken hands with the pair and they were ready to pull out.

"That was fast," said Jean, as the trailer made a right turn onto the road.

"No point prolonging it," said Jay. "She's in the best of hands."

"Who were those people?" asked Jean. "I was expecting Frances and her little girl. The one who's going to ride Chocolate."

Jay laughed.

"I'm afraid they don't have a horse trailer, honey, or even a truck. But cousin Jay has contacts. You need to in this business."

"You mean that man and young woman are going to pull a single pony in that big trailer all the way to Burlington?"

"No. They've got other horses to pick up and deliver at various locations along the way, but believe me - they don't need to worry about the gas money. It pays to have rich friends. I've done favours for them in the past, and now they're doing a favour for me.

"Well, I've got to get back to my lesson. It's a group lesson. Come and watch, if you want a good laugh."

"I think I'll go and clean out Chocolate's stall," said Jean.

"Don't bother about that. Dennis will do it."

"If it's all the same to you, I'd rather do it myself," snapped Jean peevishly. Jay looked at her in surprise, as it was uncharacteristic of her to be bad-tempered. Then he shrugged his shoulders off-handedly, and headed towards the arena.

Chapter Eight

Exhibition

The end of June had arrived and with it the annual Fairview exhibition. Jean wasn't particularly looking forward to the horse show this year since she wouldn't be riding in it. Last year she and Chocolate had won the Junior Division. This year she was just a spectator. Jay had suggested he ride Lucky Irish in the Senior Division to advance the horse's training. It would also give the O'Briens a chance to see if they wanted to purchase the horse for their daughter.

"I can hardly wait to see Lucky Irish perform," said Mrs. O'Brien.

Jean didn't let on that she would rather be riding a pony in the show herself than having her coach ride her leased horse. Nor did she mention the things that were bothering her about Lucky Irish's training program. She felt it would be ungrateful to mention her dissatisfaction to her parents after they had spent so much money on her riding.

One of the things that bothered Jean was the lack of turnout Irish received. Jay always seemed to have some reason the big fellow should be kept in his stall. He either wanted him kept in because he was going to train him later in the day, or he suspected a slight sprain, or he worried about his getting injured by the other horses before the show. It was true Irish was always extremely foolish when he *was* let out and he seemed to get easily hurt, but Jean felt it was only because his turnout was so limited. She was sure he would settle down with the other horses if he were let out more.

At the same time that Jay was keeping Irish confined most of the day, he was also feeding him large amounts of performance feed grain. This was supplied by the Pratts and Jean wondered if they were aware how much the horse was actually eating.

"We'll get him in condition in no time with this good food," Jay told Jean, but the end result of the high feed and confinement was a horse so strong and so spirited that nobody but Jay could successfully ride him.

The O'Briens met Jay and Jean at the exhibition and watched with interest as the big horse backed off the trailer. Jay had the chain of the lead line hooked onto one side of the halter and out the other side across Irish's sensitive nose. When the horse tried to act up, a quick jerk downward stopped him in his tracks.

Bridle Acres was to be represented at the show by Sandra Roland on Candy, the Tarses twins on their ponies, and Jay. Sheila Graham had quit riding after finding Jay behind the barn with Cindy.

Jean knew that with room for only four horses in the trailer, it was typical of Jay to take the twins whose parents were the richest clients at the stable.

In the pony classes, Megan and Mike Tarses swept most of the first place ribbons between them and their parents beamed proudly. They shook hands with Jay, and then took endless photographs of the two young riders with their trophies and their coach.

After the pony classes came the Junior Division, and now it was Sandra's turn to shine. Sandra had lost ten pounds in the last month and a half in an attempt to please Jay, and she had also done a lot of extra riding, often asking Jean for help. Combined with the training Jay had done on Candy, the result was a horse and rider team who could make it adequately, if not brilliantly, around a small jumping course.

Sandra left the Junior Division with an armful of second and third place ribbons, and she shot a triumphant glance at Jean who wasn't even riding in the show. She seemed to forget who it was who had offered her free advice and encouragement ever since she had started riding at Bridle Acres. Her only goal seemed to be to gain attention from Jay.

"Good work," said Jay briefly to his proud student as she returned to the trailer with Candy. "Cool her out and then put her back with a hay net and a small drink of water."

The Open division was next, and Jean had Lucky Irish saddled and ready for Jay to mount. It hadn't been easy for her to tack him up alone with the exhibition rides in plain view, but Jay had been somewhere else— watching the Junior Division, she presumed.

"Sandra did very well," she said, looking at the ribbons on the lawn chair next to the trailer.

"I guess," said Jay. "I didn't see her." When he saw the look on Jean's face, he added:

"If it had been you in there, I would have watched every jump. Never mind, kid. It will be your turn again next year—either on Irish, or on some other horse."

"I know," said Jean. She walked with Jay over to the hunter ring.

Jay had entered Lucky Irish in Open Hunter as well as Jumper. In hunter classes style counts, while in jumper classes all that matters is if the horse gets over the jump without knocking it down.

Mr. and Mrs. O'Brien brought their lawn chairs close to the fence, eager to see what the horse they were considering buying Jean could do. Meanwhile Jason was over at the rides with a friend and a pocketful of money.

The exhibition was one horse show he didn't mind attending.

In the warm-up ring Jay rode Irish with a gadget he called a "bridge"—a strap passing from one ring of the snaffle to the other over the soft part of the horse's nose. The bridge kept the bit against the roof of Irish's mouth so that he couldn't put his tongue over it.

Irish responded to the pressure of the bridge on his nose by reaching out with his head and neck and lengthening his stride, giving him the proper look of a hunter. When Jay's number was called, he had Jean quickly remove the bridge. Irish kept the longer stride when the bridge was removed, but he quickly lost some of the softness he had demonstrated when it was in place.

Jay got two fourths and a fifth in hunter hack, working hunter over fences and handy hunter over fences—classes in which the judge is looking more at the horse than the rider. In equitation on the flat and equitation over fences he placed first.

"Lucky Irish got another first!" said Mrs. O'Brien excitedly when equitation over fences was placed. She seemed to forget it was the rider and not the horse the judge was looking at in equitation classes.

"Now comes the division where your horse will really shine," said Jay to Jean with a grin, and Jean knew he was right. One thing the horse could do was jump. He might not do it stylishly or even always controllably, but he loved the height. When Jean had first faced him with a set of trot poles and asked him to trot through them, he had cleared the lot as if they were a large oxer or spread jump.

Lucky Irish came first in every jumping class up to the last one in which the height of the fences ranged from three feet to four feet with several tricky looking combinations. Jean stood alone near the out gate and pressed her knuckles to her mouth, worrying about the horse. While she didn't always like him, and she often had her heart in her mouth when she took him over jumps during her lessons, she certainly didn't want to see him get hurt.

The final class seemed an endless succession of knockdowns, falls and refusals. Meanwhile Jay put Irish over the practice jumps again and again, applying the crop liberally if he failed to bend around the turn.

"Look at that poor horse," said a young man directly behind Jean. "That Saunders needs a touch of the crop himself. Such ignorance!"

His older companion nodded.

"He's won ever jumping class so far!" said Jean hotly, coming to Jay's defense.

"Do you know him?" asked the young man, looking directly at her in a self-assured fashion. Although probably a few years younger than Jay, he was slightly taller with dark hair and brown eyes. Jean was too annoyed to notice how good-looking he was.

"Yes I know him. He's my coach. And that's the horse I lease."

She was surprised that the young man was not in the least nonplused.

"The horse has potential," he said matter-of-factly, "but he's completely untrained. He shouldn't even be jumping two feet, let alone four feet. What he needs is some basic dressage."

"He's a jumper, not a dressage horse," said Jean.

"My dear," said the older man, causing Jean to fume. "Dressage merely means `training'. Every horse should have some basic dressage before being asked to jump. It makes the horse stronger, more supple, easier to turn. Note the way the horse tilts his head around the bends. Horses who tilt their heads are either being forced to execute a figure or not being properly guided. Lack of flexibility in the right hip joint will cause the horse to lower the right ear, just as your horse is doing now. Only leg yielding can correct this problem by making the horse more flexible laterally."

It certainly sounded like the man knew what he was talking about. Not wanting to challenge someone so much older than herself, Jean turned to his friend.

"And which horse is yours?" she demanded.

"We don't have a horse here, Miss —?"

"O'Brien. Jean O'Brien."

"I'm Paul Telford and this is Werner Maxwell."

Jean shook hands with both of them and then turned to watch Jay's round. Several times she gasped as Irish rushed at the jumps, but somehow he made it clear around the entire course. When Jay was awarded the "Rider of the Day" trophy, she turned around again to get the reaction of the two men who seemed to know so much, but had no horse of their own at the show.

They probably get their knowledge out of books, she scoffed inwardly.

The two men were gone; but her mother was running excitedly towards her.

"Guess what, Jean?" said Mrs. O'Brien, giving her daughter a great big hug. "Your father has just bought your fifteenth birthday present. Lucky Irish is all yours now!"

An astounded Jean did her best to look very happy.

Chapter Nine

Not So Lucky

Jean spent the hot days of July at the stable mucking stalls, grooming, and helping Jay with the younger students. Dennis Gentry had failed to show up for work one morning and there were murmured hints of missing money. Jean felt sad to think her champion might be a thief, but his disappearance meant a summer job for her. She was pleased to be able to earn some money for Lucky Irish's expenses.

Eve was away showing in the States for three weeks and Mr. and Mrs. Pratt rarely came to the school, relying on Jay and Jean to run the lessons. Jay began to call Jean his "right-hand woman." At night he dated Cindy, and he would tell Jean all the silly things she said and did.

Jean felt she shouldn't be laughing at Cindy's expense, but when she saw the stupid way the older girl carried on when she rode, and the way she avoided anything remotely resembling work, she had a hard time feeling guilty.

"Why do you go out with her if you don't really like her?" she asked Jay once.

"I like parts of her," said Jay with a wink.

Jack Vargas had brought in two more horses off the track, and Jean knew Jay was hoping to sell one of them to Cindy for a tidy profit somewhere down the road. They weren't bad horses, but with their conformation faults they would never make the high-class show horses Jay swore they could some day be.

One Saturday Jean arrived at work glowing with excitement. She raced into the barn and found Jay tacking up one of the track Thoroughbreds for Cindy and another potential buyer to ride.

"Good. Just the person I wanted to see," said Jay. "You can hop on and give Cindy and Derek a demonstration of what Benoit can do after just a few short weeks under my expert tutelage."

"Sure," said Jean, "but first I've got some great news. My friend Karen from school is visiting relatives in Burlington next weekend, and her parents say I can go along. On Sunday they'll drive us to your cousin's farm to visit Chocolate."

Jay was uncharacteristically silent. His eyes narrowed and he looked decidedly unhappy.

"What's the matter? Aren't you pleased?"

"Actually I'm not, Jean." Jay looked so sad Jean couldn't imagine what to think.

"I'm afraid I've got some bad news, kid. I didn't want to tell you because I knew how upset you'd be. I'm sorry. I should have let you know. Chocolate got a bad case of colic one night last week and the vet didn't get to the farm in time. I'm afraid she's dead."

"No! She can't be dead!"

Jean couldn't believe what she was hearing. Tears sprang to her eyes and the two riders waiting to try out Benoit looked uncomfortable.

"I'm afraid it's true. Look, why don't you lie down in the tack room and take a little break? I'll do the demonstration on Benoit."

"I don't want to take a break."

"You want to ride?"

"Yes, I want to ride. But not Benoit. I want to ride my own horse."

She seemed near hysteria.

"Not today, Jean. He's too keyed up."

"Why is he too keyed up? Why don't you ever let

him out? You want to ride him at the Winter Fair, don't you? You don't want me to be able to handle him at all."

"Don't be ridiculous," said Jay. He looked at Cindy and the young man named Derek, and he shrugged his shoulders with a half smile. Temperamental female, his body language suggested.

With a look of determination, Jean took Irish out of his stall and began brushing him ready to ride. Irish's eyes rolled white.

"Please Jean. Don't be a fool. At least do a little halter work with him before you ride him. I promise we'll turn him out tomorrow and then I'll help you with him tomorrow afternoon."

"In the last three weeks I've only ridden my own horse twice," stormed Jean. "I get to ride all the other horses, but my own horse isn't safe enough for me. Meanwhile you're jumping him four-and-a-half feet!"

"You're right," said Jay. "I was so wrapped up in the horse because of his potential that I began to forget you're the owner. Tomorrow. I promise."

"Well, okay then. I'll just bring him out on the halter for a little ground work today."

"Good girl. Now come on, Cindy. Let's get Benoit out there and I'll show you what he can do. Maybe someday he'll be jumping four-and-a-half feet like Jean's horse."

When Jean entered the ring with Irish on a halter, she was still shedding tears at the news of Chocolate's death. It was almost impossible to accept that the lovely pony who had been so healthy a few short weeks ago was now gone. She decided she wouldn't tell her parents, just as Jay had decided not to tell her.

In the arena Jay was doing canter figure eights on Benoit with a flying change of lead. It was obvious how talented Jay was when he got off the horse and Derek rode. Derek could barely make the horse trot a figure eight, let alone canter one.

Meanwhile Lucky Irish was prancing on the lead line and Jean was having a hard time controlling him.

"You should have put the chain across his nose," called Jay. Then he gasped.

In a split second Irish had spun around on the lead line and cowkicked, and Jean collapsed like a rag doll to the ground. She lay very still in the dirt, making a terrifying sucking sound. Cindy screamed.

"Go to the house and call for an ambulance," said Jay. Cindy just stood there blankly, so Derek jumped off Benoit and handed the horse to her. Then he ran as fast as he could for help.

When the ambulance arrived, Jean was put in a stiff body jacket and lifted onto a stretcher. She drifted in and out of consciousness on the way to the hospital while the kind young attendant apologized for every bump and turn in the road.

Her parents were already in Emergency when she arrived, alerted by Jay as to what had happened. She was wheeled away for X-rays and Ultrasound, and when she heard the diagnosis she knew she wouldn't be riding for quite some time.

"Five broken ribs and a bone splint into the lung lining," said the surgeon.

"Will you have to operate?" asked Mrs. O'Brien fearfully.

"Hopefully not. We'll see." He put his hand on Jean's hand.

"Your friend from the stable says you're lucky," he said with a slight smile.

"Lucky?" Jean's speech was blurred.

"Seems the horse only had front shoes. If he'd had back shoes, you'd probably be dead!"

Chapter Ten

The Truth

For her first five days in hospital, Jean was given painkillers directly into the muscle every four hours. At the end of each four hours the painkillers would wear off and she would suffer excruciating pain. She was glad when her visitors came immediately after an injection and not immediately before one.

Mrs. Pratt came late one afternoon with flowers and a small iced cake and took Jean's hand.

"Jay sends his best wishes," she said. "He wants you to know he would visit himself, but he's very busy with the school."

It was obvious from the look on Mrs. Pratt's face that Jean wasn't the only one who found this a lame excuse.

"You know, Jean, I feel I should possibly have kept a closer eye on Jay and the horses he was buying and selling. While I know he means no harm, I think he might occasionally overmount his riders."

"Irish would have been okay for me to ride if he were let out more and given less grain," said Jean matter-of-factly. She didn't care if she *did* get Jay in trouble. He should have come to see her before now.

"Perhaps you should find out what the horse was like in the past," said Mrs. Pratt. "Get your parents to look on his registration papers and contact his previous owners. It was up to Jay to do that before he sold him to you, but I wonder if he actually did?"

After Mrs. Pratt left, Jean phoned her mother and repeated what had been said. Then she phoned Jay who told her emphatically that he didn't know anything about Irish's past behaviour since he had bought him directly from Bartons' Equestrian Centre. If he had had any suspicion whatsoever that the horse might be a kicker, he would never have let Jean buy him.

Over and over again he told Jean how sorry he was, and he promised to come and see her as soon as he got a break in his lesson schedule. He didn't mention what he was doing in the evenings that prevented him from coming.

That night, when Jean's parents came to visit, her father was in a great state of excitement.

"I tracked down your horse's previous owners," he told Jean, "and they were completely shocked to hear what had happened to you. Mr. Pammett said he told Jay the horse cowkicked and could be dangerous."

"But Jay said he bought the horse directly from the stable and didn't know anything about his past behaviour," said Jean in confusion.

"Then I guess he's lying."

"Can I talk to the Pammetts myself, Dad?"

"What for?"

"I'd like to get the whole story. I'd like to know what else Jay lied about."

"Sure. Go ahead. Just tell the operator to put the charges on our home number."

When Mr. Pammett realized whom it was he was talking to, he was extremely upset and sympathetic.

"My wife and I feel terrible about all this," he told Jean, "but we did tell Mr. Saunders the reason we were getting rid of Irish was because he kicked my wife in the knee the week before we put him up for sale. We don't know very much about horses, and he certainly wasn't the right horse for us. My wife just wanted something to use on trails. We didn't realize at the time we bought him that there's a big difference between a quiet trail horse and a highstrung Thoroughbred jumper."

"You say you told Jay that Irish kicked your wife in the knee just a week before he bought him?" asked Jean incredulously.

"I sure did. I didn't want to be responsible for somebody else's getting hurt. Jay said it was okay because he was buying the horse for himself, and he was experienced enough to handle him. It was Jay's name on the cheque—a cheque for two thousand dollars."

"Two thousand dollars? Jay said he paid three thousand dollars. Then he sold him to my parents for that amount for my birthday present. He told them he wasn't taking any commission—that he just wanted me to have a good horse!"

"I guess he *is* a good horse if you know how to deal with him," said Mr. Pammett. "He did well at the shows when he was young. Say, I've got an idea. I know the names of some dressage riders in your area who are really knowledgeable about horses. Paul Telford and Werner Maxwell. Why don't I give you their number, and maybe they can help you decide what to do with Irish?"

Jean didn't know much about the dressage riders in the area, since they were on a totally different show circuit from the hunter-jumper riders. After Jean had thanked Mr. Pammett for his help, she looked at the names on her notepad. Paul Telford and Werner Maxwell. Where had she heard those names before? Then she remembered the exhibition, and the young man who had criticized Jay's training methods.

When she told her parents what Mr. Pammett had said, they were both furious.

"We've got to get that horse away from there as soon as possible," said Mr. O'Brien. "The Pratts may be okay, but you can't stay there as long as Jay Saunders is running the show. I'm not quite sure how we're going to do it, though."

"Mr. Pammett gave me the name of someone to call," said Jean. "Why don't we wait until I'm out of here, and then we'll go and get Irish and move him to another stable?"

"I guess that's the best thing to do," said Mrs. O'Brien. "Still, I'm so mad it's going to be hard to wait. Why don't you give the person a call right now and see what he has to say?"

Jean dialled the number Mr. Pammett had given her and a young woman's voice said:

"Eastside Equestrian Centre. Can I help you?"

"I'd like to speak to a Mr. Paul Telford or a Mr. Werner Maxwell, please," said Jean.

"Werner is in Germany horse shopping," said the woman. "Hold on a moment, please. I'll get you Paul."

A few minutes later, a deep voice said hello. Jean wasn't quite sure how to begin.

"Hello," she said hesitantly. "Do you remember at the Fairview exhibition you talked to a girl about the horse that won the Open Jumper class?"

"Yes," said Paul Telford cautiously.

"Well, that's me - Jean O'Brien. The horse is Lucky Irish, and my coach sold him to my parents for three thousand dollars, and the horse kicked me and broke five of my ribs, and now I'm in the hospital, and I talked to his previous owner Mr. Pammett, and Mr. Pammett only got two thousand dollars, even though Jay said he wasn't going to take any commission, and my parents and I want to take Irish somewhere where he'll get turned out and where the people are knowledgeable, and Mr. Pammett said to phone you."

Paul Telford began to laugh.

"Well, I don't think it's very funny," said Jean angrily.

"I'm sorry, I really am, Jean. It's just that you sounded like a recording being played at the wrong speed. You're right! It's not funny at all, and I'd be glad to help you. What would you like me to do? Would you like to bring the horse here?"

Jean knew little about Eastside Equestrian Centre. She did know the centre was quite a distance from her home, and that it was primarily a dressage stable. Still, there seemed little alternative at this stage but to take Irish to Eastside. Perhaps they could sell him from there after he had been rehabilitated.

"Yes, please, if that's alright with you. We have to wait a week, though, until I'm out of hospital."

"That's really not necessary," said Paul wryly. "We're quite capable of trailering a horse by ourselves."

"Of course you are," said Jean, "but when Lucky Irish leaves Bridle Acres, I'm going to be there with him!"

Chapter Eleven

Confrontation

Jay Saunders had no warning at all that Paul Telford, Mr. O'Brien and Jean were coming one warm and rainy Saturday morning in mid-August to fetch Lucky Irish. Now that she knew just how unscrupulous he really was, Jean was afraid he might do something to her horse if he suspected what they had in mind.

When the trailer pulled into the driveway at Bridle Acres, Jay was nowhere in sight. Although it was painful for Jean to walk (it would be another full month before her bones healed completely), she was the first one to enter the barn.

Irish was pacing back and forth in his stall, and Jay was helping a pretty blonde girl of about seventeen tack up Candy. Jean wasn't familiar with the girl, but she *was* familiar with the way Jay talked in low tones directly to her as if she were the most important person in his life at the moment.

"Stick with me and you'll be riding in the Royal one day," he said. "All we have to do is to find you the right horse."

"How about Lucky Irish?" asked Jean.

Jay whirled around, obviously startled and most uncomfortable.

"Jean! What a wonderful surprise. I wasn't expecting to see you for a few weeks. Are you ready to get back in the saddle?"

54

"What do think?" snapped Jean. "Would you like to ride with five broken ribs?"

At this point Paul Telford and Mr. O'Brien came in after first opening the back of the trailer ready for loading Lucky Irish.

"Hello, Jay," said Mr. O'Brien. "Our board bill is paid for this month, right?"

"Sure," said Jay. "Is something wrong?"

"We're taking the horse out of here today."

"Taking him where?"

"To Eastside Equestrian Centre," said Paul. "Now let's get him out of that stall and bandage his legs."

Jay knew who Paul was. He also knew he would be hard to bluff.

"You take Candy out into the arena," he said to his student. "I'll be there shortly."

Once Candy and the girl were gone, Jay rushed out and blocked the horse trailer with his truck. Then he came back into the barn. He watched silently as Paul put on Irish's shipping bandages while Mr. O'Brien collected his daughter's tack. Then he brought out a pen and wrote something on a slip of paper which he handed to Mr. O'Brien.

"What's this?" demanded the older man.

"A bill for riding and training Irish while Jean was in hospital," said Jay.

"You're a fool if you think I'd pay that!" stormed Mr. O'Brien. He ripped the paper into shreds.

"Did you see that?" Jay demanded of Paul. "Did you see what he did with his bill? Unbandage that horse right now! He's not going anywhere until I'm paid."

"Oh you've been paid, young man," said Mr. O'Brien, taking a deep breath to keep himself calm. "You've been paid a thousand dollars to nearly get my daughter killed."

"I tell you I've put a lot of time and training into that horse," said Jay. "If I took a legitimate commission on a sale, that's my business. You're stupid if you think white lying doesn't go on in the horse business all the time."

"Among certain people," said Paul icily. "Tell me, did you have any sort of written agreement to train that horse?"

"No."

"I see. And who was going to show the horse? You?"

"Yes. On Jean's behalf. Everything I did was for Jean."

"Spare us any more lies," said Mr. O'Brien, taking a threatening step towards Jay. "You're just lucky I can't be bothered to sue you, young man. Now move that truck you've got parked behind the horse trailer or I might change my mind about that."

When Jean, Paul and Mr. O'Brien arrived at Eastside Equestrian Centre, Jean was amazed at how perfect everything seemed. The turnout areas were lush with grass, and the paddocks for working were beautifully fenced.

"This is lovely!" she breathed.

"Too bad it isn't a little closer to home," said Mr. O'Brien. "Still, we'll get you up here somehow if that's what you really want."

"You will? I thought we'd have to sell Irish," said Jean.

"We'll sell him if you want to get rid of him," said Mr. O'Brien. "I can't say that I'd blame you."

"Let's give him a second chance and see what he's like when he's handled properly," said Jean, and Mr. O'Brien nodded.

Paul took Irish directly to the arena where he put him on a lunge line to see exactly what they were dealing with. The horse spun to the end of the line and galloped frantically to the left.

"Tro — o — t," said Paul soothingly over and over again, playing the line as softly as if he were holding a fishing rod. Eventually the horse forgot his frenzy and began to do a relaxed trot.

"Wa — alk," said Paul, and the horse came down to a walk.

"Halt — whoa!" Irish stopped and Paul walked up to him, petting him on the shoulder and giving him a treat. When he sent the horse to the right, it was as if he were a different animal. Obediently Irish walked, trotted and cantered on command.

"That's amazing," said Mr. O'Brien. "You certainly have a way with him."

"Don't think that he's in any way reliable yet," said Paul. "The horse is willing enough, but he's in a lot of pain because of stiffness in his back and stifles. By jumping him over high jumps with no suppling exercises, Jay has made the problem even worse."

"Is he still worth keeping?" asked Jean.

"Sure he is," said Paul with a smile. "With massage and suppling exercises, reduced grain and daily turnout, he should turn into an excellent horse. If you decide to keep him, though, expect to work harder than you've ever worked before. Werner hasn't got time for students who aren't totally devoted to excellence."

"Don't you give lessons too?" asked Jean.

"I give lessons, and I take lessons. If you decide to come, Werner will give you your first lesson. If he doesn't want you as his student, he'll pass you on to me or to one of the other assistant instructors. Don't think for a moment that that will make life any easier for you!"

"I'm not looking for the easy way with Irish," said Jean. "I'm looking for the right way."

"Good. Tell that to Werner when he gets back from Germany, and you'll have a head start in getting along with him."

Paul led Irish into the barn, which was clean and orderly with wood of the finest quality. He put him in a roomy box stall with a large window, an automatic water dish, and a pile of beautiful, sweet-smelling hay in the corner.

"You can stay there until tomorrow morning, my good man," he said, giving the horse a pat. "Then we'll see how you like our special bluegrass in the small field. The next day you can be turned out with one friend, and by the end of the week you should know all the horses here. Would you like to see the other horses, Jean?"

"I'd love to."

"The boarders are outside, but the school horses are all in for the afternoon's lessons."

As Jean passed the seemingly endless stalls, she was impressed with the appearance and good nature of all the horses she saw. At the end of the second aisle were the ponies, and they were as neatly groomed and as healthy-looking as the horses.

"Nice place," said Mr. O'Brien. Then he jumped to the side as Jean let out a scream.

"Chocolate!"

Sure enough, in the second stall from the end was Jean's beloved Chocolate.

"You know her, I presume?" asked Paul with a smile.

"Know her? I used to own her! Jay told me she was dead. How did she get here?"

"There's no great mystery about it. One of our instructors, Frances Perkins, bought her from Mr. Saunders for our junior school. We ordinarily wouldn't deal with someone like that, but this mare was too good to pass up."

"Do you know what she paid for her?" asked Mr. O'Brien darkly.

"Two thousand dollars."

"And we got a thousand dollars. I can't believe he did it to us twice!"

Jean was too happy to be angry. She knew Jay must have counted on her never visiting Eastside Equestrian Centre or attending the dressage schooling shows. In fact, she undoubtedly never would have come here if Irish hadn't kicked her. Because of that kick, she had found Chocolate and could visit her any time she wanted; right now that was all that mattered.

Chapter Twelve

Lesson One

It was the first Saturday after the start of the fall school term; time for Jean's trial lesson at Eastside Equestrian Centre. Jean chewed nervously at her nails throughout the long drive to Eastside. Even though the doctor had pronounced it physically safe for her to resume riding, she was worried how she would perform in front of Werner Maxwell.

The first thing Jean did when she got out of the car was to run to the ponies in the stable and give Chocolate half a cellophane package of carrots. Then she took the other half to Lucky Irish.

"How are you feeling?" asked Paul, who had promised to attend her lesson.

"Pretty good. I've been doing the exercises the physiotherapist gave me. I just hope I haven't lost all my riding muscles."

"Werner knows how long it is since you've ridden," said Paul. "He'll be looking for horse and rider potential, not for present perfection."

"Good. You know, I'm really nervous. I feel like I'm about to take a Math exam or something."

"Try to relax. Just remember, if Werner doesn't want you as a student, I'll always take you. You probably won't be the worst student I've ever had!"

"Thanks a lot."

Jean groomed Irish carefully and then put on his saddle. The long hours she had spent lungeing him and massaging him were starting to pay off. When she tightened his girth, he hardly grouched at all.

When Jean led Irish into the arena, she could see her father give her a thumbs up through the glass of the viewing room upstairs. Paul gave her a reassuring pat on the arm before he went to the centre to take his place beside his coach. Jean prayed inwardly that her riding wouldn't embarrass the two of them.

"Mount up, please," said Mr. Maxwell quietly, and Jean sprang lightly into the saddle. She was amazed at how quickly her body had returned to normal once her bones had mended. It was hard to even remember the terrible pain of six short weeks before.

"Walk out on a loose rein."

Jean was delighted to find how much more relaxed Lucky Irish was than when she had attempted to ride him at Bridle Acres. Instead of feeling stiff all over, his back muscles swung gently as he walked, while his head was low and the long muscles on the sides of his neck were invisible on both sides.

"Remember to sit *into* the saddle and not on the saddle," said Mr. Maxwell. "Your legs should be long like the trunk of a tall pine tree. Your feet should be roots sinking down, while the top of the pine tree stretches up towards the sun."

Mr. Maxwell was in no way like Jay as a teacher. Instead of pushing her at once to try fast gaits or high jumps, he simply had her continue to walk on Lucky Irish. They did an extended walk down the sides of the arena and a collected walk at the ends. They walked in serpentines and in figure eights, and they walked across the diagonal in both directions. Then:

"You may dismount now."

Jean couldn't believe her ears. Surely she and Irish hadn't done so badly at the walk that they weren't to be given a chance to demonstrate the trot. She glanced up at her father in the viewing room, trying to hide her disappointment. He looked astonished to see her getting off the horse so soon.

"Isn't Lucky Irish any good at all?" asked Jean sadly.

"He certainly *could* be good," said Mr. Maxwell, seemingly unaware that his student felt something was wrong. "In fact, if you like, you may start lessons with me next weekend. Your lessons will be one hour in duration, and you may schedule extra lessons if your time and my time permit such scheduling."

Jean was ecstatic. She knew from Paul just how selective Mr. Maxwell was in the students he chose to teach himself. Paul smiled broadly at her now, and life seemed suddenly wonderful.

"Jean, you and your father may meet me in my office in fifteen minutes to make arrangements for your lessons," said Mr. Maxwell. "Paul, you may ride Sir Galahad now. Don't forget, Paul, the Grand Prix is only two weeks away."

Paul accompanied Jean back to the stable where he began to groom the top level dressage horse Sir Galahad ready for a training session. Sir Galahad's owner was the wealthy business magnate Herr Hansen. Herr Hansen apparently was the man who had come to pick up Chocolate at Bridle Acres while fetching horses from other, larger stables.

In his office, Mr. Maxwell made it clear to Mr. O'Brien and Jean that the road to success would in no way be easy. It would require years of dedication and many dollars worth of lessons.

"Dressage requires the systematic development of the proper muscles in both horse and rider," he said. "There are shortcut methods at the lower levels if all you want are ribbons, but success at the higher levels can come only through methodical, gymnastic training. One reason I have chosen to accept your daughter as a student, Mr. O'Brien, is that she has demonstrated through her ground work with the horse over the past several weeks a strict devotion to proper training methods. She is also a talented rider, but then so are many other young people. And you, too, have shown devotion to Jean's riding both financially and with your time in bringing her here. That's important if she plans to ride one day at a world class level."

Not at local exhibitions, but at a world class level! What an exciting thought.

"Don't forget about Paul," said Jean to Mr. Maxwell. "He's the one who showed me the proper way to work with Irish on the ground. He also taught me how to massage and groom such a sensitive horse."

"Paul thinks the horse might have a dressage show future at the lower levels," said Mr. Maxwell with a smile. "He also thinks you're a very special young lady. Now, let's get down to business. I understand from Paul that you'll be riding on your own in the evenings whenever you can get a ride to the centre. I want you to keep in mind that when you ride, you must work with a clear purpose. Aimless riding teaches neither you nor the horse anything. Practice doesn't make perfect. Only perfect practice makes perfect. Even when I'm not around and Paul's not around, I want you to execute all ring work through a disciplined and meaningful choice of exercises."

It all sounded very serious to Jean, and a bit scary—this aiming for perfection.

"But what about hacks?" she asked hesitantly, remembering the wonderful rides she once enjoyed through the fields and woods around Bridle Acres. "Do you ride cross-country here?"

"Why of course!" said Mr. Maxwell with a smile. "Hacks are excellent for relaxing horses and making them less timid. Your Lucky Irish is such a strong horse, though, I suggest you let Paul ride him on his first cross-country runs."

Mr. O'Brien saw the look of disappointment on Jean's face, a look that quickly vanished when Mr. Maxwell added:

"Perhaps you could accompany him on that school pony you admire so much—

"The pretty, bay mare called Chocolate."

Chapter Thirteen

An Old Acquaintance

By the following Saturday, Jean felt her life was as close to perfection as life could possibly get. She had just had a dressage lesson on Lucky Irish, and now she was cantering across grassy fields on a delighted Chocolate. Paul rode Lucky Irish, and he laughed as the horse jumped large over a small ditch.

"I think it's going to be a long time before he reaches what you would call a true state of relaxation," he said.

When they returned to the barn, they cooled out the horse and pony and then put them away in their stalls.

"Hi, Jean!"

Jean turned around and was astounded to see Dennis Gentry coming towards her with a wheelbarrow full of soiled shavings and manure.

"Dennis. What are you doing here?"

"New job," said Dennis, smiling. "Good people."

"But what about Bridle Acres? You just sort of disappeared." Jean didn't like to mention the rumours she had heard.

"I left because of that lying Jay Saunders," said Dennis angrily. "I knew he was a little bit crooked, but I never took him for an out-and-out thief."

"A thief? Why? What did he steal?"

"One of the boarders brought an envelope full of cash to pay for her month's board," said Dennis. "I was the only one there at the time. I told her to put it on the stall door, and I'd tell Eve it was there. It was just before

Eve went down to the States."

"And did you tell Eve?"

I couldn't find her right away," said Dennis. "Then, when I came back, I saw Jay getting into his car. I *know* he had the envelope in his hand."

"So what happened then?"

Dennis was almost crying with frustration.

"I was accused of taking the money, so I ran away. I didn't take it. Honest, I didn't. You believe me, don't you, Jean?"

"Yes, I do. I'm afraid Jay proved himself dishonest once too often for me to doubt that he would steal some money."

"Anyway, he's gone now."

"Gone?"

"Yeah. The Pratts fired him. Something to do with the sale of some horses—including yours, I think. You won't go back to Bridle Acres now he's left the district, will you?"

"No, definitely not. I like it right here."

"Good. I don't have a lot of friends, you know, so it's nice to see a familiar face."

"You'll make friends soon enough at Eastside," said Jean. "Like you said, they're good people here. Right Paul?"

"Right!" said Paul, who was passing by with a young filly he was taking to the arena for some ground training.

"Good people and nice horses," Dennis agreed quietly, almost to himself. "You know, maybe for once in my life, everything's going to be okay."

"I hope it will, Dennis," said Jean. "I really hope it will."

Québec, Canada
2000